The Indiscreet Letter

Eleanor Hallowell Abbott

Contents

THE INDISCREET LETTER...7

THE INDISCREET LETTER

BY

Eleanor Hallowell Abbott

THE INDISCREET LETTER

The Railroad Journey was very long and slow. The Traveling Salesman was rather short and quick. And the Young Electrician who lolled across the car aisle was neither one length nor another, but most inordinately flexible, like a suit of chain armor.

More than being short and quick, the Traveling Salesman was distinctly fat and unmistakably dressy in an ostentatiously new and pure-looking buff-colored suit, and across the top of the shiny black sample-case that spanned his knees he sorted and re-sorted with infinite earnestness a large and varied consignment of "Ladies' Pink and Blue Ribbed Undervests." Surely no other man in the whole southward-bound Canadian train could have been at once so ingenuous and so nonchalant.

There was nothing dressy, however, about the Young Electrician. From his huge cowhide boots to the lead smouch that ran from his rough, square chin to the very edge of his astonishingly blond curls, he was one delicious mess of toil and old clothes and smiling, blue-eyed indifference. And every time that he shrugged his shoulders or crossed his knees he jingled and jangled incongruously among his coil-boxes and insulators, like some splendid young Viking of old, half blacked up for a modern minstrel show.

More than being absurdly blond and absurdly messy, the Young Electrician had one of those extraordinarily sweet, extraordinarily vital, strangely mysterious, utterly unexplainable masculine faces that fill your senses with an odd, impersonal disquietude, an itching unrest, like the hazy, teasing reminder of some previous existence in a prehistoric cave, or, more tormenting still, with the tingling, psychic prophecy of some amazing emotional experience yet to come. The sort of face, in fact, that almost inevitably flares up into a woman's startled vision at the one crucial moment in her life when she is not supposed to be considering alien features.

Out from the servient shoulders of some smooth-tongued Waiter it stares, into the scared dilating pupils of the White Satin Bride with her pledged hand clutching her Bridegroom's sleeve. Up from the gravelly, pick-and-shovel labor of the new-made grave it lifts its weirdly magnetic eyes to the Widow's tears. Down from some petted Princeling's silver-trimmed saddle horse it smiles its electrifying, wistful smile into the Peasant's sodden weariness. Across the slender white rail of an always *out-going* steamer it stings back into your gray, land-locked consciousness like the tang of a scarlet spray. And the secret of the face, of course, is "Lure"; but to save your soul you could not decide in any specific case whether the lure is the lure of personality, or the lure of physiognomy--a mere accidental, coincidental, haphazard harmony of forehead and cheek-bone and twittering facial muscles.

Something, indeed, in the peculiar set of the Young Electrician's jaw warned you quite definitely that if you should ever even so much as hint the small, sentimental word "lure" to him he would most certainly "swat" you on first impulse for a maniac, and on second impulse for a liar--smiling at you all the while in the strange little wrinkly tissue round his eyes.

The voice of the Railroad Journey was a dull, vague, conglomerate, cinder-scented babble of grinding wheels and shuddering window frames; but the voices of the Traveling Salesman and the Young Electrician were shrill, gruff, poignant, inert, eternally variant, after the manner of human voices which are discussing the affairs of the universe.

"Every man," affirmed the Traveling Salesman sententiously--"every man has written one indiscreet letter during his lifetime!"

"Only one?" scoffed the Young Electrician with startling distinctness above even the loudest roar and rumble of the train.

With a rather faint, rather gaspy chuckle of amusement the Youngish

Girl in the seat just behind the Traveling Salesman reached forward then and touched him very gently on the shoulder.

"Oh, please, may I listen?" she asked quite frankly.

With a smile as benevolent as it was surprised, the Traveling Salesman turned half-way around in his seat and eyed her quizzically across the gold rim of his spectacles.

"Why, sure you can listen!" he said.

The Traveling Salesman was no fool. People as well as lisle thread were a specialty of his. Even in his very first smiling estimate of the Youngish Girl's face, neither vivid blond hair nor luxuriantly ornate furs misled him for an instant. Just as a Preacher's high waistcoat passes him, like an official badge of dignity and honor, into any conceivable kind of a situation, so also does a woman's high forehead usher her with delicious impunity into many conversational experiences that would hardly be wise for her lower-browed sister.

With an extra touch of manners the Salesman took off his neat brown derby hat and placed it carefully on the vacant seat in front of him. Then, shifting his sample-case adroitly to suit his new twisted position, he began to stick cruel little prickly price marks through alternate meshes of pink and blue lisle.

"Why, sure you can listen!" he repeated benignly. "Traveling alone's awful stupid, ain't it? I reckon you were glad when the busted heating apparatus in the sleeper gave you a chance to come in here and size up a few new faces. Sure you can listen! Though, bless your heart, we weren't talking about anything so very specially interesting," he explained conscientiously. "You see, I was merely arguing with my young friend here that if a woman really loves you, she'll follow you through any kind of blame or disgrace--follow you anywheres, I said--anywheres!"

"Not anywheres," protested the Young Electrician with a grin. "'Not up a telegraph pole!'" he requoted sheepishly.

"Y-e-s--I heard that," acknowledged the Youngish Girl with blithe shamelessness.

"Follow you 'anywheres,' was what I said," persisted the Traveling Salesman almost irritably. "Follow you 'anywheres'! Run! Walk! Crawl on her hands and knees if it's really necessary. And yet--" Like a shaggy brown line drawn across the bottom of a column of figures, his eyebrows narrowed to their final calculation. "And yet--" he estimated cautiously, "and yet--there's times when I ain't so almighty sure that her following you is any more specially flattering to you than if you was a burglar. She don't follow you so much, I reckon, because you *are* her love as because you've **got** her love. God knows it ain't just you, yourself, she's afraid of losing. It's what she's already invested in you that's worrying her! All her pinky-posy, cunning kid-dreams about loving and marrying, maybe; and the pretty-much grown-up winter she fought out the whisky question with you, perhaps; and the summer you had the typhoid, likelier than not; and the spring the youngster was born-- oh, sure, the spring the youngster was born! Gee! If by swallowing just one more yarn you tell her, she can only keep on holding down all the old yarns you ever told her--if, by forgiving you just one more forgive-you, she can only hang on, as it were, to the original worth-whileness of the whole darned business--if by--"

"Oh, that's what you meant by the 'whole darned business,' was it?" cried the Youngish Girl suddenly, edging away out to the front of her seat. Along the curve of her cheeks an almost mischievous smile began to quicken. "Oh, yes! I heard that, too!" she confessed cheerfully. "But what was the beginning of it all? The very beginning? What was the first thing you said? What started you talking about it? Oh, please, excuse me for hearing anything at all," she finished abruptly; "but I've been traveling alone now for five dreadful days, all the way down from British Columbia, and--if--you--will--persist--in-- saying interesting things--in trains--you must take the consequences!"

There was no possible tinge of patronage or condescension in her voice, but rather, instead, a bumpy, naive sort of friendliness, as lonesome Royalty sliding temporarily down from its throne might reasonably contend with each bump, "A King may look at a cat! He may! He may!"

Along the edge of the Young Electrician's cheek-bones the red began to flush furiously. He seemed to have a funny little way of blushing just before he spoke, and the physical mannerism gave an absurdly italicized sort of emphasis to even the most trivial thing that he said.

"I guess you'll have to go ahead and tell her about 'Rosie,'" he suggested grinningly to the Traveling Salesman.

"Yes! Oh, do tell me about 'Rosie,'" begged the Youngish Girl with whimsical eagerness. "Who in creation was 'Rosie'?" she persisted laughingly. "I've been utterly mad about 'Rosie' for the last half-hour!"

"Why, 'Rosie' is nobody at all--probably," said the Traveling Salesman a trifle wryly.

"Oh, pshaw!" flushed the Young Electrician, crinkling up all the little smile-tissue around his blue eyes. "Oh, pshaw! Go ahead and tell her about 'Rosie.'"

"Why, I tell you it wasn't anything so specially interesting," protested the Traveling Salesman diffidently. "We simply got jollying a bit in the first place about the amount of perfectly senseless, no-account truck that'll collect in a fellow's pockets; and then some sort of a scorched piece of paper he had, or something, got him telling me about a nasty, sizzling close call he had to-day with a live wire; and then I got telling him here about a friend of mine--and a mighty good fellow, too--who dropped dead on the street one day last summer with an unaddressed, typewritten letter in his pocket that began 'Dearest Little Rosie,' called her a 'Honey' and a 'Dolly Girl' and a 'Pink-Fingered Precious,' made a rather foolish dinner appointment for Thursday in New Haven, and was signed--in the Lord's own time--at the end of four pages, 'Yours forever, and then some. TOM.'--Now the wife of the deceased was named--Martha."

Quite against all intention, the Youngish Girl's laughter rippled out explosively and caught up the latent amusement in the Young Electrician's face. Then, just as unexpectedly, she wilted back a little into her seat.

"I don't call that an 'indiscreet letter'!" she protested almost resentfully.

"You might call it a knavish letter. Or a foolish letter. Because either a knave or a fool surely wrote it! But 'indiscreet'? U-m-m, No!"

"Well, for heaven's sake!" said the Traveling Salesman. "If--you--don't--call--that--an--indiscreet letter, what would you call one?"

"Yes, sure," gasped the Young Electrician, "what would you call one?" The way his lips mouthed the question gave an almost tragical purport to it.

"What would I call an 'indiscreet letter'?" mused the Youngish Girl slowly. "Why--why--I think I'd call an 'indiscreet letter' a letter that was pretty much--of a gamble perhaps, but a letter that was perfectly, absolutely legitimate for you to send, because it would be your own interests and your own life that you were gambling with, not the happiness of your wife or the honor of your husband. A letter, perhaps, that might be a trifle risky--but a letter, I mean, that is absolutely on the square!"

"But if it's absolutely 'on the square,'" protested the Traveling Salesman, worriedly, "then where in creation does the 'indiscreet' come in?"

The Youngish Girl's jaw dropped. "Why, the 'indiscreet' part comes in," she argued, "because you're not able to prove in advance, you know, that the stakes you're gambling for are absolutely 'on the square.' I don't know exactly how to express it, but it seems somehow as though only the very little things of Life are offered in open packages--that all the big things come sealed very tight. You can poke them a little and make a guess at the shape, and you can rattle them a little and make a guess at the size, but you can't ever open them and prove them--until the money is paid down and gone forever from your hands. But goodness me!" she cried, brightening perceptibly; "if you were to put an advertisement in the biggest newspaper in the biggest city in the world, saying: 'Every person who has ever written an indiscreet letter in his life is hereby invited to attend a mass-meeting'--and if people would really go--you'd see the most distinguished public gathering that you ever saw in your life! Bishops and Judges and Statesmen and Beautiful Society Women and Little Old White-Haired Mothers--everybody, in fact, who had ever had red blood enough at least once in his life to write down in cold black and white the one vital, quivering, questioning fact that happened to mean the most to him at that moment! But your 'Honey' and your 'Dolly Girl' and your 'Pink-Fingered Precious' nonsense! Why, it isn't real! Why, it doesn't even *make sense*!"

Again the Youngish Girl's laughter rang out in light, joyous, utterly superficial appreciation.

Even the serious Traveling Salesman succumbed at last.

"Oh, yes, I know it sounds comic," he acknowledged wryly. "Sounds like something out of a summer vaudeville show or a cheap Sunday supplement. But I don't suppose it sounded so specially blamed comic to the widow. I reckon she found it plenty-heap indiscreet enough to suit her. Oh, of course," he added hastily, "I know, and Martha knows that Thomkins wasn't at all that kind of a fool. And yet, after all--when you really settle right down to think about it, Thomkins' name was easily 'Tommy,' and Thursday sure enough was his day in New Haven, and it was a yard of red flannel that Martha had asked him to bring home to her--not the scarlet automobile veil that they found in his pocket. But 'Martha,' I says, of course, 'Martha, it sure does beat all how we fellows that travel round so much in cars and trains are always and forever picking up automobile veils--dozens of them, *dozens*--red, blue, pink, yellow--why, I wouldn't wonder if my wife had as many as thirty-four tucked away in her top bureau drawer!'--'I wouldn't wonder,' says Martha, stooping lower and lower over Thomkins's blue cotton shirt that she's trying to cut down into rompers for the baby. 'And, Martha,' I says, 'that letter is just a joke. One of the boys sure put it up on him!'--'Why, of course,' says Martha, with her mouth all puckered up crooked, as though a kid had stitched it on the machine. 'Why, of course! How dared you think--'"

Forking one bushy eyebrow, the Salesman turned and stared quizzically off into space.

"But all the samey, just between you and I," he continued judicially, "all the samey, I'll wager you anything you name that it ain't just death that's pulling Martha down day by day, and night by night, limper and lanker and clumsier-footed. Martha's got a sore thought. That's what ails her. And God help the crittur with a sore thought! God help anybody who's got any one single, solitary sick idea that keeps thinking on top of itself, over and over and over, boring into the past, bumping into the future, fussing, fretting, eternally festering. Gee! Compared to it, a tight shoe is easy slippers, and water dropping on your head is perfect peace!--Look close at Martha, I say. Every night when the blowsy old moon shines like courting time, every day when the butcher's bill comes home as big as a swollen elephant, when the crippled stepson tries to cut his throat again, when the youngest kid sneezes funny like his father--'WHO WAS ROSIE? WHO WAS ROSIE?'"

"Well, who was Rosie?" persisted the Youngish Girl absent-mindedly.

"Why, Rosie was *nothing*!" snapped the Traveling Salesman; "nothing at all--probably." Altogether in spite of himself, his voice trailed off into a suspiciously minor key. "But all the same," he continued more vehemently, "all the same--it's just that little darned word 'probably' that's making all the mess and bother of it--because, as far as I can reckon, a woman can stand absolutely anything under God's heaven that she knows; but she just up and can't stand the littlest, teeniest, no-account sort of thing that she ain't sure of. Answers may kill 'em dead enough, but it's questions that eats 'em alive."

For a long, speculative moment the Salesman's gold-rimmed eyes went frowning off across the snow-covered landscape. Then he ripped off his glasses and fogged them very gently with his breath.

"Now--I--ain't--any--saint," mused the Traveling Salesman meditatively, "and I--ain't very much to look at, and being on the road ain't a business that would exactly enhance my valuation in the eyes of a lady who was actually looking out for some safe place to bank her affections; but I've never yet reckoned on running with any firm that didn't keep up to its advertising promises, and if a man's courtship ain't his own particular, personal advertising proposition--then I don't know anything about--anything! So if I should croak sudden any time in a railroad accident or a hotel fire or a scrap in a saloon, I ain't calculating on leaving my wife any very large amount of 'sore thoughts.' When a man wants his memory kept green, he don't mean--gangrene!

"Oh, of course," the Salesman continued more cheerfully, "a sudden croaking leaves any fellow's affairs at pretty raw ends--lots of queer, bitter-tasting things that would probably have been all right enough if they'd only had time to get ripe. Lots of things, I haven't a doubt, that would make my wife kind of mad, but nothing, I'm calculating, that she wouldn't understand. There'd be no questions coming in from the office, I mean, and no fresh talk from the road that she ain't got the information on hand to meet. Life insurance ain't by any means, in my mind, the only kind of protection that a man owes his widow. Provide for her Future--if you can!--That's my motto!--But a man's just a plain bum who don't provide for his own Past! She may have plenty of trouble in the years to come settling her own bills, but she ain't going to have any worry settling any of mine. I tell you, there'll be no ladies swelling round in crape at my funeral that my wife don't know by their first names!"

With a sudden startling guffaw the Traveling Salesman's mirth rang joyously out above the roar of the car.

"Tell me about your wife," said the Youngish Girl a little wistfully.

Around the Traveling Salesman's generous mouth the loud laugh flickered down to a schoolboy's bashful grin.

"My wife?" he repeated. "Tell you about my wife? Why, there isn't much to tell. She's little. And young. And was a school-teacher. And I married her four years ago."

"And were happy--ever--after," mused the Youngish Girl teasingly.

"No!" contradicted the Traveling Salesman quite frankly. "No! We didn't find out how to be happy at all until the last three years!"

Again his laughter rang out through the car.

"Heavens! Look at me!" he said at last. "And then think of her!--Little, young, a school-teacher, too, and taking poetry to read on the train same as you or I would take a newspaper! Gee! What would you expect?" Again his mouth began to twitch a little. "And I thought it was her fault--'most all of the first year," he confessed delightedly. "And then, all of a sudden," he continued eagerly, "all of a sudden, one day, more mischievous-spiteful than anything else, I says to her, 'We don't seem to be getting on so very well, do we?' And she shakes her head kind of slow. 'No, we don't!' she says.--'Maybe you think I don't treat you quite right?' I quizzed, just a bit mad.--'No, you don't! That is, not--exactly right,' she says, and came burrowing her head in my shoulder as cozy as could be.--'Maybe you could show me how to treat you--righter,' I says, a little bit pleasanter.--'I'm perfectly sure I could!' she says, half laughing and half crying. 'All you'll have to do,' she says, 'is just to watch me!'--'Just watch what *you* do?' I said, bristling just a bit again.--'No,' she says, all pretty and soft-like; 'all I want you to do is to watch what I ***don't*** do!'"

With slightly nervous fingers the Traveling Salesman reached up and tugged at his necktie as though his collar were choking him suddenly.

"So that's how I learned my table manners," he grinned, "and that's how I learned to quit cussing when I was mad round the house, and that's how I learned--oh, a great many things--and that's how I learned--" grinning broader and broader--"that's how I learned not to come home and talk all the time about the 'peach' whom I saw on the train or the street. My wife, you see, she's got a little scar on her face--it don't show any, but she's awful sensitive about it, and 'Johnny,' she says, 'don't you never notice that I don't ever rush home and tell *you* about the wonderful *slim* fellow who sat next to me at the theater, or the simply elegant *grammar* that I heard at the lecture? I can recognize a slim fellow when I see him, Johnny,' she says, 'and I like nice grammar as well as the next one, but praising 'em to you, dear, don't seem to me so awfully polite. Bragging about handsome women to a plain wife, Johnny,' she says, 'is just about as raw as bragging about rich men to a husband who's broke.'

"Oh, I tell you a fellow's a fool," mused the Traveling Salesman judicially, "a fellow's a fool when he marries who don't go to work deliberately to study and understand his wife. Women are awfully understandable if you only go at it right. Why, the only thing that riles them in the whole wide world is the fear that the man they've married ain't quite bright. Why, when I was first married I used to think that my wife was awful snippety about other women. But, Lord! when you point a girl out in the car and say, 'Well, ain't that girl got the most gorgeous head of hair you ever saw in your life?' and your wife says: 'Yes--Jordan is selling them puffs six for a dollar seventy-five this winter,' she ain't intending to be snippety at all. No!--It's only, I tell you, that it makes a woman feel just plain silly to think that her husband don't even know as much as she does. Why, Lord! she don't care how much you praise the grocer's daughter's style, or your stenographer's spelling, as long as you'll only show that you're *equally wise* to the fact that the grocer's daughter sure has a nasty temper, and that the stenographer's spelling is mighty near the best thing about her.

"Why, a man will go out and pay every cent he's got for a good hunting dog--and then snub his wife for being the finest untrained retriever in the world. Yes, sir, that's what she is--a retriever; faithful, clever, absolutely unscarable, with no other object in life except to track down and fetch to her husband every possible interesting fact in the world that he don't already know. And then she's so excited and pleased with what she's got in her mouth that it 'most breaks her heart if her man don't seem to care about it. Now, the secret of training her lies in the fact that she won't never trouble to hunt out and fetch you any news that she sees you already know. And just as soon as a man once appreciates all this--then Joy is come to the Home!

"Now there's Ella, for instance," continued the Traveling Salesman thoughtfully. "Ella's a traveling man, too. Sells shotguns up through the Aroostook. Yes, shotguns! Funny, ain't it, and me selling undervests? Ella's an awful smart girl. Good as gold. But cheeky? Oh, my!--Well, once I would have brought her down to the house for Sunday, and advertised her as a 'peach,' and a 'dandy good fellow,' and praised her eyes, and bragged about her cleverness, and generally done my best to smooth over all her little deficiencies with as much palaver as I could. And that little retriever of mine would have gone straight to work and ferreted out every single, solitary, un-complimentary thing about Ella that she could find, and 'a' fetched 'em to me as pleased and proud as a puppy, expecting, for all the world, to be petted and patted for her astonishing shrewdness. And there would sure have been gloom in the Sabbath.

"But now--now--what I say now is: 'Wife, I'm going to bring Ella down for Sunday. You've never seen her, and you sure will hate her. She's big, and showy, and just a little bit rough sometimes, and she rouges her cheeks too much, and she's likelier than not to chuck me under the chin. But it would help your old man a lot in a business way if you'd be pretty nice to her. And I'm going to send her down here Friday, a day ahead of me.'--And oh, gee!--I ain't any more than jumped off the car Saturday night when there's my little wife out on the street corner with her sweater tied over her head, prancing up and down first on one foot and then on the other--she's so excited, to slip her hand in mine and tell me all about it. 'And Johnny,' she says--even be-fore I've got my glove off--'Johnny,' she says, 'really, do you know, I think you've done Ella an injustice. Yes, truly I do. Why, she's *just as kind*! And she's shown me how to cut my last year's coat over into the nicest sort of a little spring jacket! And she's made us a chocolate cake as big as a dish-pan. Yes, she has! And Johnny, don't you dare tell her that I told you--but do you know she's putting her brother's boy through Dartmouth? And you old Johnny Clifford, I don't care a darn whether she rouges a little bit or not--and you oughtn't to care--either! So there!'"

With sudden tardy contrition the Salesman's amused eyes wandered to the open book on the Youngish Girl's lap.

"I sure talk too much," he muttered. "I guess maybe you'd like half a chance to read your story."

The expression on the Youngish Girl's face was a curious mixture of hu-mor and seriousness. "There's no special object in reading," she said, "when you can hear a bright man talk!"

As unappreciatingly as a duck might shake champagne from its back, the Traveling Salesman shrugged the compliment from his shoulders.

"Oh, I'm bright enough," he grumbled, "but I ain't refined." Slowly to the tips of his ears mounted a dark red flush of real mortification.

"Now, there's some traveling men," he mourned, "who are as slick and fine as any college president you ever saw. But me? I'd look coarse sipping warm milk out of a gold-lined spoon. I haven't had any education. And I'm fat, besides!" Almost plaintively he turned and stared for a second from the Young Electrician's embarrassed grin to the Youngish Girl's more subtle smile. "Why, I'm nearly fifty years old," he said, "and since I was fifteen the only learning I've ever got was what I picked up in trains talking to whoever sits nearest to me. Sometimes it's hens I learn about. Sometimes it's national politics. Once a young Canuck farmer sitting up all night with me coming down from St. John learned me all about the French Revolution. And now and then high school kids will give me a point or two on astronomy. And in this very seat I'm sitting in now, I guess, a red-kerchiefed Dago woman, who worked on a pansy farm just outside of Boston, used to ride in town with me every night for a month, and she coached me quite a bit on Dago talk, and I paid her five dollars for that."

"Oh, dear me!" said the Youngish Girl, with unmistakable sincerity. "I'm afraid you haven't learned anything at all from me!"

"Oh, yes, I have too!" cried the Traveling Salesman, his whole round face lighting up suddenly with real pleasure. "I've learned about an entirely new kind of lady to go home and tell my wife about. And I'll bet you a hundred dollars that you're a good deal more of a 'lady' than you'd even be willing to tell us. There ain't any provincial-- 'Don't-you-dare-speak-to-me--this-is-the-first-time-I-ever-was-on-a-train air about you! I'll bet you've traveled a lot--all round the world--froze your eyes on icebergs and scorched 'em some on tropics."

"Y-e-s," laughed the Youngish Girl.

"And I'll bet you've met the Governor-General at least once in your life."

"Yes," said the Girl, still laughing. "He dined at my house with me a week ago yesterday."

"And I'll bet you, most of anything," said the Traveling Salesman shrewdly, "that you're haughtier than haughty with folks of your own kind. But with people like us--me and the Electrician, or the soldier's widow from South Africa who does your washing, or the Eskimo man at the circus--you're as simple as a kitten. All your own kind of folks are nothing but grown-up people to you, and you treat 'em like grown-ups all right--a hundred cents to the dollar--but all our kind of folks are *playmates* to you, and you take us as easy and pleasant as you'd slide down on the floor and play with any other kind of a kid. Oh, you can tackle the other proposition all right--dances and balls and general gold lace glories; but it ain't fine loafers sitting round in parlors talking about the weather that's going to hold you very long, when all the time your heart's up and over the back fence with the kids who are playing the games. And, oh, say!" he broke off abruptly--"would you think it awfully impertinent of me if I asked you how you do your hair like that? 'Cause, surer than smoke, after I get home and supper is over and the dishes are washed and I've just got to sleep, that little wife of mine will wake me up and say: 'Oh, just one thing more. How did that lady in the train do her hair?'"

With her chin lifting suddenly in a burst of softly uproarious delight, the Youngish Girl turned her head half-way around and raised her narrow, black-gloved hands to push a tortoise-shell pin into place.

"Why, it's perfectly simple," she explained. "It's just three puffs, and two curls, and then a twist."

"And then a twist?" quizzed the Traveling Salesman earnestly, jotting down the memorandum very carefully on the shiny black surface of his sample-case. "Oh, I hope I ain't been too familiar," he added, with sudden contriteness. "Maybe I ought to have introduced myself first. My name's Clifford. I'm a drummer for Sayles & Sayles. Maine and the Maritime Provinces--that's my route. Boston's the home office. Ever been in Halifax?" he quizzed a trifle proudly. "Do an awful big business in Halifax! Happen to know the Emporium store? The London, Liverpool, and Halifax Emporium?"

The Youngish Girl bit her lip for a second before she answered. Then, very quietly, "Y-e-s," she said, "I know the Emporium--slightly. That is--I-- own the block that the Emporium is in."

"Gee!" said the Traveling Salesman. "Oh, gee! Now I *know* I talk too much!"

In nervously apologetic acquiescence the Young Electrician reached up a lean, clever, mechanical hand and smouched one more streak of black across his forehead in a desperate effort to reduce his tousled yellow hair to the particular smoothness that befitted the presence of a lady who owned a business block in any city whatsoever.

"My father owned a store in Malden, once," he stammered, just a trifle wistfully, "but it burnt down, and there wasn't any insurance. We always were a powerfully unlucky family. Nothing much ever came our way!"

Even as he spoke, a toddling youngster from an overcrowded seat at the front end of the car came adventuring along the aisle after the swaying, clutching manner of tired, fretty children on trains. Hesitating a moment, she stared up utterly unsmilingly into the Salesman's beaming face, ignored the Youngish Girl's inviting hand, and with a sudden little chuckling sigh of contentment, climbed up clumsily into the empty place beside the Young Electrician, rummaged bustlingly around with its hands and feet for an instant, in a petulant effort to make a comfortable nest for itself, and then snuggled down at last, lolling half-way across the Young Electrician's perfectly strange knees, and drowsed off to sleep with all the delicious, friendly, unconcerned sang-froid of a tired puppy. Almost unconsciously the Young Electrician reached out and unfastened the choky collar of the heavy, sweltering little overcoat; yet not a glance from his face had either lured or caressed the strange child for a single second. Just for a moment, then, his smiling eyes reassured the jaded, jabbering French-Canadian mother, who turned round with craning neck from the front of the car.

"She's all right here. Let her alone!" he signaled gesticulatingly from child to mother.

Then, turning to the Traveling Salesman, he mused reminiscently: "Talking's--all--right. But where in creation do you get the time to *think*? Got any kids?" he asked abruptly.

"N-o," said the Traveling Salesman. "My wife, I guess, is kid enough for me."

Around the Young Electrician's eyes the whimsical smile-wrinkles deepened with amazing vividness. "Huh!" he said. "I've got six."

"Gee!" chuckled the Salesman. "Boys?"

The Young Electrician's eyebrows lifted in astonishment. "Sure they're boys!" he said. "Why, of course!"

The Traveling Salesman looked out far away through the window and whistled a long, breathy whistle. "How in the deuce are you ever going to take care of 'em?" he asked. Then his face sobered suddenly. "There was only two of us fellows at home--just Daniel and me--and even so--there weren't ever quite enough of anything to go all the way round."

For just an instant the Youngish Girl gazed a bit skeptically at the Traveling Salesman's general rotund air of prosperity.

"You don't look--exactly like a man who's never had enough," she said smilingly.

"Food?" said the Traveling Salesman. "Oh, shucks! It wasn't food I was thinking of. It was education. Oh, of course," he added conscientiously, "of course, when the crops weren't either too heavy or too blooming light, Pa usually managed some way or other to get Daniel and me to school. And schooling was just nuts to me, and not a single nut so hard or so green that I wouldn't have chawed and bitten my way clear into it. But Daniel--Daniel somehow couldn't seem to see just how to enter a mushy Bartlett pear without a knife or a fork--in some other person's fingers. He was all right, you know--but he just couldn't seem to find his own way alone into anything. So when the time came--" the grin on the Traveling Salesman's mouth grew just a little bit wry at one corner--"and so when the time came--it was an awful nice, sweet-smelling June night, I remember, and I'd come home early--I walked into the kitchen as nice as pie, where Pa was sitting dozing in the cat's rocking-chair, in his gray stocking feet, and I threw down before him my full year's school report. It was pink, I remember, which was supposed to be the rosy color of success in our school; and I says: 'Pa! There's my report! And Pa,' I says, as bold and stuck-up as a brass weathercock on a new church, 'Pa! Teacher says that one of your boys has got to go to college!' And I was grinning all the while, I remember, worse than any Chessy cat.

"And Pa he took my report in both his horny old hands and he spelt it all out real careful and slow and respectful, like as though it had been a lace valentine, and 'Good boy!' he says, and 'Bully boy!' and 'So Teacher says that one of my boys has got to go to college? One of my boys? Well, which one? Go fetch me Daniel's report.' So I went and fetched him Daniel's report. It was gray, I remember--the supposed color of failure in our school--and I stood with the grin still half frozen on my face while Pa spelt out the dingy record of poor Daniel's year. And then, 'Oh, gorry!' says Pa. 'Run away and g'long to bed. I've got to think. But first,' he says, all suddenly cautious and thrifty, 'how much does it cost to go to college?' And just about as delicate and casual as a missionary hinting for a new chapel, I blurted out loud as a bull: 'Well, if I go up state to our own college, and get a chance to work for part of my board, it will cost me just $255 a year, or maybe--maybe,' I stammered, 'maybe, if I'm extra careful, only $245.50, say. For four years that's only $982,' I finished triumphantly.

"'G-a-w-d!' says Pa. Nothing at all except just, 'G-a-w-d!'

"When I came down to breakfast the next morning, he was still sitting there in the cat's rocking-chair, with his face as gray as his socks, and all the rest of him--blue jeans. And my pink school report, I remember, had slipped down under the stove, and the tortoise-shell cat was lashing it with her tail; but Daniel's report, gray as his face, was still clutched up in Pa's horny old hand. For just a second we eyed each other sort of dumb-like, and then for the first time, I tell you, I seen tears in his eyes.

"'Johnny,' he says, 'it's Daniel that'll have to go to college. Bright men,' he says, 'don't need no education.'"

Even after thirty years the Traveling Salesman's hand shook slightly with the memory, and his joggled mind drove him with unwonted carelessness to pin price mark after price mark in the same soft, flimsy mesh of pink lisle. But the grin on his lips did not altogether falter.

"I'd had pains before in my stomach," he acknowledged good-naturedly, "but that morning with Pa was the first time in my life that I ever had any pain in my plans!--So we mortgaged the house and the cow-barn and the maple-sugar trees," he continued, more and more cheerfully, "and Daniel finished his schooling--in the Lord's own time--and went to college."

With another sudden, loud guffaw of mirth all the color came flushing back again into his heavy face.

"Well, Daniel has sure needed all the education he could get," he affirmed heartily. "He's a Methodist minister now somewhere down in Georgia--and, educated 'way up to the top notch, he don't make no more than $650 a year. $650!--oh, glory! Why, Daniel's piazza on his new house cost him $175, and his wife's last hospital bill was $250, and just one dentist alone gaffed him sixty-five dollars for straightening his oldest girl's teeth!"

"Not sixty-five?" gasped the Young Electrician in acute dismay. "Why, two of my kids have got to have it done! Oh, come now--you're joshing!"

"I'm not either joshing," cried the Traveling Salesman. "Sure it was sixty-five dollars. Here's the receipted bill for it right here in my pocket." Brusquely he reached out and snatched the paper back again. "Oh, no, I beg your pardon. That's the receipt for the piazza.--What? It isn't? For the hospital bill then?--Oh, hang! Well, never mind. It *was* sixty-five dollars. I tell you I've got it somewhere."

"Oh--you--paid--for--them--all, did you?" quizzed the Youngish Girl before she had time to think.

"No, indeed!" lied the Traveling Salesman loyally. "But $650 a year? What can a family man do with that? Why, I earned that much before I was twenty-one! Why, there wasn't a moment after I quit school and went to work that I wasn't earning real money! From the first night I stood on a street corner with a gasoline torch, hawking rasin-seeders, up to last night when I got an eight-hundred-dollar raise in my salary, there ain't been a single moment in my life when I couldn't have sold you my boots; and if you'd buncoed my boots away from me I'd have sold you my stockings; and if you'd buncoed my stockings away from me I'd have rented you the privilege of jumping on my bare toes. And I ain't never missed a meal yet--though once in my life I was forty-eight hours late for one!--Oh, I'm bright enough," he mourned, "but I tell you I ain't refined."

With the sudden stopping of the train the little child in the Young Electrician's lap woke fretfully. Then, as the bumpy cars switched laboriously into a siding, and the engine went puffing off alone on some noncommittal errand of its own, the Young Electrician rose and stretched himself and peered out of the window into the acres and acres of snow, and bent down suddenly and swung the child to his shoulder, then, sauntering down the aisle to the door, jumped off into the snow and started to explore the edge of a little, snow-smothered pond which a score of red-mittened children were trying frantically to clear with huge yellow brooms. Out from the crowd of loafers that hung about the station a lean yellow hound came nosing aimlessly forward, and then suddenly, with much fawning and many capers, annexed itself to the Young Electrician's heels like a dog that has just rediscovered its long-lost master. Halfway up the car the French Canadian mother and her brood of children crowded their faces close to the window--and thought they were watching the snow.

And suddenly the car seemed very empty. The Youngish Girl thought it was her book that had grown so astonishingly devoid of interest. Only the Traveling Salesman seemed to know just exactly what was the matter. Craning his neck till his ears reddened, he surveyed and resurveyed the car, complaining: "What's become of all the folks?"

A little nervously the Youngish Girl began to laugh. "Nobody has gone," she said, "except--the Young Electrician."

With a grunt of disbelief the Traveling Salesman edged over to the window and peered out through the deepening frost on the pane. Inquisitively the Youngish Girl followed his gaze. Already across the cold, white, monotonous, snow-smothered landscape the pale afternoon light was beginning to wane, and against the lowering red and purple streaks of the wintry sunset the Young Electrician's figure, with the little huddling pack on its shoulder, was silhouetted vaguely, with an almost startling mysticism, like the figure of an unearthly Traveler starting forth upon an unearthly journey into an unearthly West.

"Ain't he the nice boy!" exclaimed the Traveling Salesman with almost passionate vehemence.

"Why, I'm sure I don't know!" said the Youngish Girl a trifle coldly. "Why--it would take me quite a long time--to decide just how--nice he was. But--" with a quick softening of her voice--"but he certainly makes one think of--nice things--Blue Mountains, and Green Forests, and Brown Pine Needles, and a Long, Hard Trail, shoulder to shoulder--with a chance to warm one's heart at last at a hearth-fire--bigger than a sunset!"

Altogether unconsciously her small hands went gripping out to the edge of her seat, as though just a grip on plush could hold her imagination back from soaring into a miraculous, unfamiliar world where women did not idle all day long on carpets waiting for men who came on--pavements.

"Oh, my God!" she cried out with sudden passion. "I wish I could have lived just one day when the world was new. I wish--I wish I could have reaped just one single, solitary, big Emotion before the world had caught it and--appraised it--and taxed it--and licensed it--and *staled* it!"

"Oh-ho!" said the Traveling Salesman with a little sharp indrawing of his breath. "Oh-ho!--So that's what the--Young Electrician makes you think of, is it?"

For just an instant the Traveling Salesman thought that the Youngish

Girl was going to strike him.

"I wasn't thinking of the Young Electrician at all!" she asserted angrily. "I was thinking of something altogether--different."

"Yes. That's just it," murmured the Traveling Salesman placidly. "Something--altogether--different. Every time I look at him it's the darnedest thing! Every time I look at him I--forget all about him. My head begins to wag and my foot begins to tap--and I find myself trying to--hum him--as though he was the words of a tune I used to know."

When the Traveling Salesman looked round again, there were tears in the Youngish Girl's eyes, and an instant after that her shoulders went plunging forward till her forehead rested on the back of the Traveling Salesman's seat.

But it was not until the Young Electrician had come striding back to his seat, and wrapped himself up in the fold of a big newspaper, and not until the train had started on again and had ground out another noisy mile or so, that the Traveling Salesman spoke again--and this time it was just a little bit surreptitiously.

"What--you--crying--for?" he asked with incredible gentleness.

"I don't know, I'm sure," confessed the Youngish Girl, snuffingly. "I guess I must be tired."

"U-m-m," said the Traveling Salesman.

After a moment or two he heard the sharp little click of a watch.

"Oh, dear me!" fretted the Youngish Girl's somewhat smothered voice. "I didn't realize we were almost two hours late. Why, it will be dark, won't it, when we get into Boston?"

"Yes, sure it will be dark," said the Traveling Salesman.

After another moment the Youngish Girl raised her forehead just the merest trifle from the back of the Traveling Salesman's seat, so that her voice sounded distinctly more definite and cheerful. "I've--never--been--to--Boston--before," she drawled a little casually.

"What!" exclaimed the Traveling Salesman. "Been all around the world-

-and never been to Boston?--Oh, I see," he added hurriedly, "you're afraid your friends won't meet you!"

Out of the Youngish Girl's erstwhile disconsolate mouth a most surprising laugh issued. "No! I'm afraid they *will* meet me," she said dryly.

Just as a soldier's foot turns from his heel alone, so the Traveling Salesman's whole face seemed to swing out suddenly from his chin, till his surprised eyes stared direct into the Girl's surprised eyes.

"My heavens!" he said. "You don't mean that *you've*--been writing an--'indiscreet letter'?"

"Y-e-s--I'm afraid that I have," said the Youngish Girl quite blandly. She sat up very straight now and narrowed her eyes just a trifle stubbornly toward the Traveling Salesman's very visible astonishment. "And what's more," she continued, clicking at her watch-case again--"and what's more, I'm on my way now to meet the consequences of said indiscreet letter.'"

"Alone?" gasped the Traveling Salesman.

The twinkle in the Youngish Girl's eyes brightened perceptibly, but the firmness did not falter from her mouth.

"Are people apt to go in--crowds to--meet consequences?" she asked, perfectly pleasantly.

"Oh--come, now!" said the Traveling Salesman's most persuasive voice. "You don't want to go and get mixed up in any sensational nonsense and have your picture stuck in the Sunday paper, do you?"

The Youngish Girl's manner stiffened a little. "Do I look like a person who gets mixed up in sensational nonsense?" she demanded rather sternly.

"N-o-o," acknowledged the Traveling Salesman conscientiously. "N-o-o; but then there's never any telling what you calm, quiet-looking, still-waters sort of people will go ahead and do--once you get started." Anxiously he took out his watch, and then began hurriedly to pack his samples back into his case. "It's only twenty-five minutes more," he argued earnestly. "Oh, I say now, don't you go off and do anything foolish! My wife will be down at the station to meet me. You'd like my wife. You'd like her fine!--Oh, I say now, you come home with us for Sunday, and think things over a bit."

As delightedly as when the Traveling Salesman had asked her how she fixed her hair, the Youngish Girl's hectic nervousness broke into genuine laughter. "Yes," she teased, "I can see just how pleased your wife would be to have you bring home a perfectly strange lady for Sunday!"

"My wife is only a kid," said the Traveling Salesman gravely, "but she likes what I like--all right--and she'd give you the shrewdest, eagerest little 'helping hand' that you ever got in your life--if you'd only give her a chance to help you out--with whatever your trouble is."

"But I haven't any 'trouble,'" persisted the Youngish Girl with brisk cheerfulness. "Why, I haven't any trouble at all! Why, I don't know but what I'd just as soon tell you all about it. Maybe I really ought to tell somebody about it. Maybe--anyway, it's a good deal easier to tell a stranger than a friend. Maybe it would really do me good to hear how it sounds out loud. You see, I've never done anything but whisper it--just to myself--before. Do you remember the wreck on the Canadian Pacific Road last year? Do you? Well--I was in it!"

"Gee!" said the Traveling Salesman. "'Twas up on just the edge of Canada, wasn't it? And three of the passenger coaches went off the track? And the sleeper went clear over the bridge? And fell into an awful gully? And caught fire besides?"

"Yes," said the Youngish Girl. "I was in the sleeper."

Even without seeming to look at her at all, the Traveling Salesman could see quite distinctly that the Youngish Girl's knees were fairly knocking together and that the flesh around her mouth was suddenly gray and drawn, like an old person's. But the little persistent desire to laugh off everything still flickered about the corners of her lips.

"Yes," she said, "I was in the sleeper, and the two people right in front of me were killed; and it took almost three hours, I think, before they got any of us out. And while I was lying there in the darkness and mess and everything, I cried--and cried--and cried. It wasn't nice of me, I know, nor brave, nor anything, but I couldn't seem to help it--underneath all that pile of broken seats and racks and beams and things.

"And pretty soon a man's voice--just a voice, no face or anything, you know, but just a voice from somewhere quite near me, spoke right out and said: 'What in creation are you crying so about? Are you awfully hurt?' And I said--though I didn't mean to say it at all, but it came right out--'N-o, I don't think I'm hurt, but I don't like having all these seats and windows piled on top of me,' and I began crying all over again. 'But no one else is crying,' reproached the Voice.--'And there's a perfectly good reason why not,' I said. 'They're all dead!'--'O--h,' said the Voice, and then I began to cry harder than ever, and principally this time, I think, I cried because the horrid, old red plush cushions smelt so stale and dusty, jammed against my nose.

"And then after a long time the Voice spoke again and it said, 'If I'll sing you a little song, will you stop crying?' And I said, 'N-o, I don't think I could!' And after a long time the Voice spoke again, and it said, 'Well, if I'll tell you a story will you stop crying?' And I considered it a long time, and finally I said, 'Well, if you'll tell me a perfectly true story--a story that's never, never been told to any one before--I'll try and stop!'

"So the Voice gave a funny little laugh almost like a woman's hysterics, and I stopped crying right off short, and the Voice said, just a little bit mockingly: 'But the only perfectly true story that I know--the only story that's never--never been told to anybody before is the story of my life.' 'Very well, then,' I said, 'tell me that! Of course I was planning to live to be very old and learn a little about a great many things; but as long as apparently I'm not going to live to even reach my twenty-ninth birthday--to-morrow--you don't know how unutterably it would comfort me to think that at least I knew *everything* about some one thing!'

"And then the Voice choked again, just a little bit, and said: 'Well--here goes, then. Once upon a time--but first, can you move your right hand? Turn it just a little bit more this way. There! Cuddle it down! Now, you see, I've made a little home for it in mine. Ouch! Don't press down too hard! I think my wrist is broken. All ready, then? You won't cry another cry? Promise? All right then. Here goes. Once upon a time--'

"Never mind about the story," said the Youngish Girl tersely. "It began about the first thing in all his life that he remembered seeing--something funny about a grandmother's brown wig hung over the edge of a white piazza railing--and he told me his name and address, and all about his people, and all about his business, and what banks his money was in, and something about some land down in the Panhandle, and all the bad things that he'd ever done in his life, and all the good things, that he wished there'd been more of, and all the things that no one would dream of telling you if he ever, ever expected to see Daylight again--things so intimate--things so--

"But it wasn't, of course, about his story that I wanted to tell you. It was about the 'home,' as he called it, that his broken hand made for my--frightened one. I don't know how to express it; I can't exactly think, even, of any words to explain it. Why, I've been all over the world, I tell you, and fairly loafed and lolled in every conceivable sort of ease and luxury, but the Soul of me--the wild, restless, breathless, discontented *soul* of me--never sat down before in all its life--I say, until my frightened hand cuddled into his broken one. I tell you I don't pretend to explain it, I don't pretend to account for it; all I know is--that smothering there under all that horrible wreckage and everything--the instant my hand went home to his, the most absolute sense of serenity and contentment went over me. Did you ever see young white horses straying through a white-birch wood in the springtime? Well, it felt the way that *looks*!--Did you ever hear an alto voice singing in the candle-light? Well, it felt the way that *sounds*! The last vision you would like to glut your eyes on before blindness smote you! The last sound you would like to glut your ears on before deafness dulled you! The last touch--before Intangibility! Something final, complete, supreme--ineffably satisfying!

"And then people came along and rescued us, and I was sick in the hospital for several weeks. And then after that I went to Persia. I know it sounds silly, but it seemed to me as though just the smell of Persia would be able to drive away even the memory of red plush dust and scorching woodwork. And there was a man on the steamer whom I used to know at home--a man who's almost always wanted to marry me. And there was a man who joined our party at Teheran--who liked me a little. And the land was like silk and silver and attar of roses. But all the time I couldn't seem to think about anything except how perfectly awful it was that a *stranger* like me should be running round loose in the world, carrying all the big, scary secrets of a man who didn't even know where I was. And then it came to me all of a sudden, one rather worrisome day, that no woman who knew as much about a man as I did was exactly a 'stranger' to him. And then, twice as suddenly, to great, grown-up, cool-blooded, money-staled, book-tamed *me*--it swept over me like a cyclone that I should never be able to decide anything more in all my life--not the width of a tinsel ribbon, not the goal of a journey, not the worth of a lover--until I'd seen the Face that belonged to the Voice in the railroad wreck.

"And I sat down--and wrote the man a letter--I had his name and address, you know. And there--in a rather maddening moonlight night on the Caspian Sea--all the horrors and terrors of that other--Canadian night came back to me and swamped completely all the arid timidity and sleek conventionality that women like me are hidebound with all their lives, and I wrote him--that unknown, unvisualized, unimagined--MAN--the utterly free, utterly frank, utterly honest sort of letter that any brave soul would write any other brave soul--every day of the world--if there wasn't any flesh. It wasn't a love letter. It wasn't even a sentimental letter. Never mind what I told him. Never mind anything except that there, in that tropical night on a moonlit sea, I asked him to meet me here, in Boston, eight months afterward--on the same Boston-bound Canadian train--on this--the anniversary of our other tragic meeting."

"And you think he'll be at the station?" gasped the Traveling Salesman.

The Youngish Girl's answer was astonishingly tranquil. "I don't know, I'm sure," she said. "That part of it isn't my business. All I know is that I wrote the letter--and mailed it. It's Fate's move next."

"But maybe he never got the letter!" protested the Traveling Salesman, buckling frantically at the straps of his sample-case.

"Very likely," the Youngish Girl answered calmly. "And if he never got it, then Fate has surely settled everything perfectly definitely for me--that way. The only trouble with that would be," she added whimsically, "that an unanswered letter is always pretty much like an unhooked hook. Any kind of a gap is apt to be awkward, and the hook that doesn't catch in its own intended tissue is mighty apt to tear later at something you didn't want torn."

"I don't know anything about that," persisted the Traveling Salesman, brushing nervously at the cinders on his hat. "All I say is--maybe he's married."

"Well, that's all right," smiled the Youngish Girl. "Then Fate would have settled it all for me perfectly satisfactorily *that* way. I wouldn't mind at all his not being at the station. And I wouldn't mind at all his being married. And I wouldn't mind at all his turning out to be very, very old. None of those things, you see, would interfere in the slightest with the memory of the--Voice or the--chivalry of the broken hand. THE ONLY THING I'D MIND, I TELL YOU, WOULD BE TO THINK THAT HE REALLY AND TRULY WAS THE MAN WHO WAS MADE FOR ME--AND I MISSED FINDING IT OUT!-- Oh, of course, I've worried myself sick these past few months thinking of the audacity of what I've done. I've got such a 'Sore Thought,' as you call it, that I'm almost ready to scream if anybody mentions the word 'indiscreet' in my presence. And yet, and yet--after all, it isn't as though I were reaching out into the darkness after an indefinite object. What I'm reaching out for is a *light*, so that I can tell exactly just what object is there. And, anyway," she quoted a little waveringly:

"He either fears his fate too much,
Or his, deserts are small,
Who dares not put it to the touch

To gain or lose it all!"

"Ain't you scared just a little bit?" probed the Traveling Salesman.

All around them the people began bustling suddenly with their coats and bags. With a gesture of impatience the Youngish Girl jumped up and started to fasten her furs. The eyes that turned to answer the Traveling Salesman's question were brimming wet with tears.

"Yes--I'm--scared to death!" she smiled incongruously.

Almost authoritatively the Salesman reached out his empty hand for her traveling-bag. "What you going to do if he ain't there?" he asked.

The Girl's eyebrows lifted. "Why, just what I'm going to do if he *is* there," she answered quite definitely. "I'm going right back to Montreal to-night. There's a train out again, I think, at eight-thirty. Even late as we are, that will give me an hour and a half at the station."

"Gee!" said the Traveling Salesman. "And you've traveled five days just to see what a man looks like--for an hour and a half?"

"I'd have traveled twice five days," she whispered, "just to see what he looked like--for a--second and a half!"

"But how in thunder are you going to recognize him?" fussed the Traveling Salesman. "And how in thunder is he going to recognize you?"

"Maybe I won't recognize him," acknowledged the Youngish Girl, "and likelier than not he won't recognize me; but don't you see?--can't you understand?--that all the audacity of it, all the worry of it--is absolutely nothing compared to the one little chance in ten thousand that we *will* recognize each other?"

"Well, anyway," said the Traveling Salesman stubbornly, "I'm going to walk out slow behind you and see you through this thing all right."

"Oh, no, you're not!" exclaimed the Youngish Girl. "Oh, no, you're not! Can't you see that if he's there, I wouldn't mind you so much; but if he doesn't come, can't you understand that maybe I'd just as soon you didn't know about it?"

"O-h," said the Traveling Salesman.

A little impatiently he turned and routed the Young Electrician out of his sprawling nap. "Don't you know Boston when you see it?" he cried a trifle testily.

For an instant the Young Electrician's sleepy eyes stared dully into the Girl's excited face. Then he stumbled up a bit awkwardly and reached out for all his coil-boxes and insulators.

"Good-night to you. Much obliged to you," he nodded amiably.

A moment later he and the Traveling Salesman were forging their way ahead through the crowded aisle. Like the transient, impersonal, altogether mysterious stimulant of a strain of martial music, the Young Electrician vanished into space. But just at the edge of the car steps the Traveling Salesman dallied a second to wait for the Youngish Girl.

"Say," he said, "say, can I tell my wife what you've told me?"

"Y-e-s," nodded the Youngish Girl soberly.

"And say," said the Traveling Salesman, "say, I don't exactly like to go off this way and never know at all how it all came out." Casually his eyes fell on the big lynx muff in the Youngish Girl's hand. "Say," he said, "if I promise, honest-Injun, to go 'way off to the other end of the station, couldn't you just lift your muff up high, once, if everything comes out the way you want it?"

"Y-e-s," whispered the Youngish Girl almost inaudibly.

Then the Traveling Salesman went hurrying on to join the Young Electrician, and the Youngish Girl lagged along on the rear edge of the crowd like a bashful child dragging on the skirts of its mother.

Out of the groups of impatient people that flanked the track she saw a dozen little pecking reunions, where some one dashed wildly into the long, narrow stream of travelers and yanked out his special friend or relative, like a good-natured bird of prey. She saw a tired, worn, patient-looking woman step forward with four noisy little boys, and then stand dully waiting while the Young Electrician gathered his riotous offspring to his breast. She saw the Traveling Salesman grin like a bashful school-boy, just as a red-cloaked girl came running to him and bore him off triumphantly toward the street.

And then suddenly, out of the blur, and the dust, and the dizziness, and the half-blinding glare of lights, the figure of a Man loomed up directly and indomitably across the Youngish Girl's path--a Man standing bare-headed and faintly smiling as one who welcomes a much-reverenced guest--a Man tall, stalwart, sober-eyed, with a touch of gray at his temples, a Man whom any woman would be proud to have waiting for her at the end of any journey. And right there before all that hurrying, scurrying, self-centered, unseeing crowd, he reached out his hands to her and gathered her frightened fingers close into his.

"You've--kept--me--waiting--a--long--time," he reproached her.

"Yes!" she stammered. "Yes! Yes! The train was two hours late!"

"It wasn't the hours that I was thinking about," said the Man very quietly. "It was the--year!"

And then, just as suddenly, the Youngish Girl felt a tug at her coat, and, turning round quickly, found herself staring with dazed eyes into the eager, childish face of the Traveling Salesman's red-cloaked wife. Not thirty feet away from her the Traveling Salesman's shameless, stolid-looking back seemed to be blocking up the main exit to the street.

"Oh, are you the lady from British Columbia?" queried the excited little voice. Perplexity, amusement, yet a divine sort of marital confidence were in the question.

"Yes, surely I am," said the Youngish Girl softly.

Across the little wife's face a great rushing, flushing wave of tenderness blocked out for a second all trace of the cruel, slim scar that marred the perfect contour of one cheek.

"Oh, I don't know at all what it's all about," laughed the little wife, "but my husband asked me to come back and kiss you!"

The Codes Of Hammurabi And Moses
W. W. Davies

QTY

The discovery of the Hammurabi Code is one of the greatest achievements of archaeology, and is of paramount interest, not only to the student of the Bible, but also to all those interested in ancient history...

Religion   ISBN: *1-59462-338-4*   **Pages:132**
                                                MSRP $12.95

The Theory of Moral Sentiments
Adam Smith

QTY

This work from 1749. contains original theories of conscience amd moral judgment and it is the foundation for systemof morals.

Philosophy ISBN: *1-59462-777-0*   **Pages:536**
                                                MSRP $19.95

Jessica's First Prayer
Hesba Stretton

QTY

In a screened and secluded corner of one of the many railway-bridges which span the streets of London there could be seen a few years ago, from five o'clock every morning until half past eight, a tidily set-out coffee-stall, consisting of a trestle and board, upon which stood two large tin cans, with a small fire of charcoal burning under each so as to keep the coffee boiling during the early hours of the morning when the work-people were thronging into the city on their way to their daily toil...

Childrens   ISBN: *1-59462-373-2*   **Pages:84**
                                                MSRP $9.95

My Life and Work
Henry Ford

QTY

Henry Ford revolutionized the world with his implementation of mass production for the Model T automobile. Gain valuable business insight into his life and work with his own auto-biography... "We have only started on our development of our country we have not as yet, with all our talk of wonderful progress, done more than scratch the surface. The progress has been wonderful enough but..."

Biographies/ ISBN: *1-59462-198-5*   **Pages:300**
                                                MSRP $21.95

The Art of Cross-Examination
Francis Wellman

QTY

I presume it is the experience of every author, after his first book is published upon an important subject, to be almost overwhelmed with a wealth of ideas and illustrations which could readily have been included in his book, and which to his own mind, at least, seem to make a second edition inevitable. Such certainly was the case with me; and when the first edition had reached its sixth impression in five months, I rejoiced to learn that it seemed to my publishers that the book had met with a sufficiently favorable reception to justify a second and considerably enlarged edition. ..

Pages:412

Reference   **ISBN: *1-59462-647-2***   *MSRP $19.95*

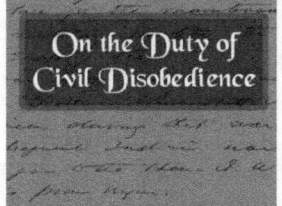

On the Duty of Civil Disobedience
Henry David Thoreau

QTY

Thoreau wrote his famous essay, On the Duty of Civil Disobedience, as a protest against an unjust but popular war and the immoral but popular institution of slave-owning. He did more than write—he declined to pay his taxes, and was hauled off to gaol in consequence. Who can say how much this refusal of his hastened the end of the war and of slavery ?

Law   **ISBN: *1-59462-747-9***   **Pages:48**

MSRP $7.45

Dream Psychology Psychoanalysis for Beginners
Sigmund Freud

QTY

Sigmund Freud, born Sigismund Schlomo Freud (May 6, 1856 - September 23, 1939), was a Jewish-Austrian neurologist and psychiatrist who co-founded the psychoanalytic school of psychology. Freud is best known for his theories of the unconscious mind, especially involving the mechanism of repression; his redefinition of sexual desire as mobile and directed towards a wide variety of objects; and his therapeutic techniques, especially his understanding of transference in the therapeutic relationship and the presumed value of dreams as sources of insight into unconscious desires.

Pages:196

Psychology   **ISBN: *1-59462-905-6***   *MSRP $15.45*

The Miracle of Right Thought
Orison Swett Marden

QTY

Believe with all of your heart that you will do what you were made to do. When the mind has once formed the habit of holding cheerful, happy, prosperous pictures, it will not be easy to form the opposite habit. It does not matter how improbable or how far away this realization may see, or how dark the prospects may be, if we visualize them as best we can, as vividly as possible, hold tenaciously to them and vigorously struggle to attain them, they will gradually become actualized, realized in the life. But a desire, a longing without endeavor, a yearning abandoned or held indifferently will vanish without realization.

Pages:360

Self Help   **ISBN: *1-59462-644-8***   *MSRP $25.45*

www.bookjungle.com *email: sales@bookjungle.com fax: 630-214-0564 mail: Book Jungle PO Box 2226 Champaign, IL 61825*

QTY

The Rosicrucian Cosmo-Conception Mystic Christianity *by Max Heindel*   ISBN: *1-59462-188-8*   **$38.95**
The Rosicrucian Cosmo-conception is not dogmatic, neither does it appeal to any other authority than the reason of the student. It is: not controversial, but is: sent forth in the, hope that it may help to clear...   New Age/Religion Pages 646

Abandonment To Divine Providence *by Jean-Pierre de Caussade*   ISBN: *1-59462-228-0*   **$25.95**
"The Rev. Jean Pierre de Caussade was one of the most remarkable spiritual writers of the Society of Jesus in France in the 18th Century. His death took place at Toulouse in 1751. His works have gone through many editions and have been republished...   Inspirational/Religion Pages 400

Mental Chemistry *by Charles Haanel*   ISBN: *1-59462-192-6*   **$23.95**
Mental Chemistry allows the change of material conditions by combining and appropriately utilizing the power of the mind. Much like applied chemistry creates something new and unique out of careful combinations of chemicals the mastery of mental chemistry...   New Age Pages 354

The Letters of Robert Browning and Elizabeth Barret Barrett 1845-1846 vol II   ISBN: *1-59462-193-4*   **$35.95**
by Robert Browning and Elizabeth Barrett   Biographies Pages 596

Gleanings In Genesis (volume I) *by Arthur W. Pink*   ISBN: *1-59462-130-6*   **$27.45**
Appropriately has Genesis been termed "the seed plot of the Bible" for in it we have, in germ form, almost all of the great doctrines which are afterwards fully developed in the books of Scripture which follow...   Religion/Inspirational Pages 420

The Master Key *by L. W. de Laurence*   ISBN: *1-59462-001-6*   **$30.95**
In no branch of human knowledge has there been a more lively increase of the spirit of research during the past few years than in the study of Psychology, Concentration and Mental Discipline. The requests for authentic lessons in Thought Control, Mental Discipline and...   New Age/Business Pages 422

The Lesser Key Of Solomon Goetia *by L. W. de Laurence*   ISBN: *1-59462-092-X*   **$9.95**
This translation of the first book of the "Lernegton" which is now for the first time made accessible to students of Talismanic Magic was done, after careful collation and edition, from numerous Ancient Manuscripts in Hebrew, Latin, and French...   New Age/Occult Pages 92

Rubaiyat Of Omar Khayyam *by Edward Fitzgerald*   ISBN: *1-59462-332-5*   **$13.95**
Edward Fitzgerald, whom the world has already learned, in spite of his own efforts to remain within the shadow of anonymity, to look upon as one of the rarest poets of the century, was born at Bredfield, in Suffolk, on the 31st of March, 1809. He was the third son of John Purcell...   Music Pages 172

Ancient Law *by Henry Maine*   ISBN: *1-59462-128-4*   **$29.95**
The chief object of the following pages is to indicate some of the earliest ideas of mankind, as they are reflected in Ancient Law, and to point out the relation of those ideas to modern thought.   Religion/History Pages 452

Far-Away Stories *by William J. Locke*   ISBN: *1-59462-129-2*   **$19.45**
"Good wine needs no bush, but a collection of mixed vintages does. And this book is just such a collection. Some of the stories I do not want to remain buried for ever in the museum files of dead magazine-numbers an author's not unpardonable vanity..."   Fiction Pages 272

Life of David Crockett *by David Crockett*   ISBN: *1-59462-250-7*   **$27.45**
"Colonel David Crockett was one of the most remarkable men of the times in which he lived. Born in humble life, but gifted with a strong will, an indomitable courage, and unremitting perseverance...   Biographies/New Age Pages 424

Lip-Reading *by Edward Nitchie*   ISBN: *1-59462-206-X*   **$25.95**
Edward B. Nitchie, founder of the New York School for the Hard of Hearing, now the Nitchie School of Lip-Reading, Inc, wrote "LIP-READING Principles and Practice". The development and perfecting of this meritorious work on lip-reading was an undertaking...   How-to Pages 400

A Handbook of Suggestive Therapeutics, Applied Hypnotism, Psychic Science   ISBN: *1-59462-214-0*   **$24.95**
by Henry Munro   Health/New Age/Health/Self-help Pages 376

A Doll's House: and Two Other Plays *by Henrik Ibsen*   ISBN: *1-59462-112-8*   **$19.95**
Henrik Ibsen created this classic when in revolutionary 1848 Rome. Introducing some striking concepts in playwriting for the realist genre, this play has been studied the world over.   Fiction/Classics/Plays 308

The Light of Asia *by sir Edwin Arnold*   ISBN: *1-59462-204-3*   **$13.95**
In this poetic masterpiece, Edwin Arnold describes the life and teachings of Buddha. The man who was to become known as Buddha to the world was born as Prince Gautama of India but he rejected the worldly riches and abandoned the reigns of power when...   Religion/History/Biographies Pages 170

The Complete Works of Guy de Maupassant *by Guy de Maupassant*   ISBN: *1-59462-157-8*   **$16.95**
"For days and days, nights and nights, I had dreamed of that first kiss which was to consecrate our engagement, and I knew not on what spot I should put my lips..."   Fiction/Classics Pages 240

The Art of Cross-Examination *by Francis L. Wellman*   ISBN: *1-59462-309-0*   **$26.95**
Written by a renowned trial lawyer, Wellman imparts his experience and uses case studies to explain how to use psychology to extract desired information through questioning.   How-to/Science/Reference Pages 408

Answered or Unanswered? *by Louisa Vaughan*   ISBN: *1-59462-248-5*   **$10.95**
Miracles of Faith in China   Religion Pages 112

The Edinburgh Lectures on Mental Science (1909) *by Thomas*   ISBN: *1-59462-008-3*   **$11.95**
This book contains the substance of a course of lectures recently given by the writer in the Queen Street Hall, Edinburgh. Its purpose is to indicate the Natural Principles governing the relation between Mental Action and Material Conditions...   New Age/Psychology Pages 148

Ayesha *by H. Rider Haggard*   ISBN: *1-59462-301-5*   **$24.95**
Verily and indeed it is the unexpected that happens! Probably if there was one person upon the earth from whom the Editor of this, and of a certain previous history, did not expect to hear again...   Classics Pages 380

Ayala's Angel *by Anthony Trollope*   ISBN: *1-59462-352-X*   **$29.95**
The two girls were both pretty, but Lucy who was twenty-one who supposed to be simple and comparatively unattractive, whereas Ayala was credited, as her Bombwhat romantic name might show, with poetic charm and a taste for romance. Ayala when her father died was nineteen...   Fiction Pages 484

The American Commonwealth *by James Bryce*   ISBN: *1-59462-286-8*   **$34.45**
An interpretation of American democratic political theory. It examines political mechanics and society from the perspective of Scotsman James Bryce   Politics Pages 572

Stories of the Pilgrims *by Margaret P. Pumphrey*   ISBN: *1-59462-116-0*   **$17.95**
This book explores pilgrims religious oppression in England as well as their escape to Holland and eventual crossing to America on the Mayflower, and their early days in New England...   History Pages 268

QTY

The Fasting Cure *by Sinclair Upton*   ISBN: *1-59462-222-1* **$13.95**
In the Cosmopolitan Magazine for May, 1910, and in the Contemporary Review (London) for April, 1910, I published an article dealing with my experi-ences in fasting. I have written a great many magazine articles, but never one which attracted so much attention... New Age/Self Help/Health Pages 164

Hebrew Astrology *by Sepharial*   ISBN: *1-59462-308-2* **$13.45**
In these days of advanced thinking it is a matter of common observation that we have left many of the old landmarks behind and that we are now pressing forward to greater heights and to a wider horizon than that which represented the mind-content of our progenitors... Astrology Pages 144

Thought Vibration or The Law of Attraction in the Thought World   ISBN: *1-59462-127-6* **$12.95**
by William Walker Atkinson   Psychology/Religion Pages 144

Optimism *by Helen Keller*   ISBN: *1-59462-108-X* **$15.95**
Helen Keller was blind, deaf, and mute since 19 months old, yet famously learned how to overcome these handicaps, communicate with the world, and spread her lectures promoting optimism. An inspiring read for everyone... Biographies/Inspirational Pages 84

Sara Crewe *by Frances Burnett*   ISBN: *1-59462-360-0* **$9.45**
In the first place, Miss Minchin lived in London. Her home was a large, dull, tall one, in a large, dull square, where all the houses were alike, and all the sparrows were alike, and where all the door-knockers made the same heavy sound... Childrens/Classic Pages 88

The Autobiography of Benjamin Franklin *by Benjamin Franklin*   ISBN: *1-59462-135-7* **$24.95**
The Autobiography of Benjamin Franklin has probably been more extensively read than any other American historical work, and no other book of its kind has had such ups and downs of fortune. Franklin lived for many years in England, where he was agent... Biographies/History Pages 332

Name	
Email	
Telephone	
Address	
City, State ZIP	

☐ **Credit Card**   ☐ **Check / Money Order**

Credit Card Number	
Expiration Date	
Signature	

Please Mail to: Book Jungle
PO Box 2226
Champaign, IL 61825
or Fax to: 630-214-0564

ORDERING INFORMATION

web*: www.bookjungle.com*
email*: sales@bookjungle.com*
fax*: 630-214-0564*
mail*: Book Jungle PO Box 2226 Champaign, IL 61825*
or PayPal *to sales@bookjungle.com*

Please contact us for bulk discounts

DIRECT-ORDER TERMS

**20% Discount if You Order
Two or More Books**
Free Domestic Shipping!
Accepted: Master Card, Visa,
Discover, American Express